Ladybird books are widely available, but in case of difficulty may be ordered by post or telephone from:
Ladybird Books – Cash Sales Department Littlegate Road Paignton Devon TQ3 3BE Telephone 0803 554761

A catalogue record for this book is available from the British Library

Published by Ladybird Books Ltd Loughborough Leicestershire UK
LADYBIRD and the device of a Ladybird are trademarks of Ladybird Books Ltd

Printed in Belgium

The sun came up over the African plain, hot and brilliant, just as it had done since the beginning of time.

But today the first rays of the morning sun shone down on an astonishing sight. Animals moved in a grand parade across the vast Pride Lands.

Elephants plodded, antelope ran, giraffes loped and cheetahs raced. Ants marched in an orderly line, while flocks of flamingos winged across the sky.

They were all travelling to Pride Rock to celebrate the birth of the Lion King's son.

Above the gathering, on a flat-topped rock, Rafiki, the ancient baboon, approached King Mufasa and Queen Sarabi. He cracked open a gourd and, with its juice, made a special mark on the tiny cub's forehead. Then he carried the cub to the edge of the rock. Holding him high, Rafiki proclaimed: "We welcome Simba, our future king, to the Circle of Life!"

Cheers rose from the plain as all the animals joined in the welcome. Then, together, they knelt before their new prince.

That afternoon Zazu, the King's adviser, flew to another part of Pride Rock to see Mufasa's brother, Scar.

"You'd better have a good excuse for missing this morning's ceremony," said Zazu. "You should have been first in line!"

"I *was* first in line – for the throne!" snarled Scar. "Then that hairball Simba came along and spoilt my chances!" Scar began to walk away in disgust.

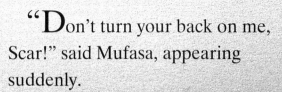

"Don't turn your back on me, Scar!" said Mufasa, appearing suddenly.

Scar whirled round. "Maybe *you* shouldn't turn your back on *me*, Mufasa!" he growled.

"Is that a challenge?" asked Mufasa.

Scar didn't answer. He just walked away, leaving Zazu and Mufasa troubled and concerned.

The days passed and Simba grew from an infant into a lively, happy cub. One morning, just as the sun was rising, Mufasa took him to the top of Pride Rock. The vast African plain lay before them.

"Simba, look," said Mufasa. "Everything the light touches is our kingdom. Some day it will all be yours."

"It's enormous, Father!" said Simba. "Do you think I'll be able to rule it all?"

"Yes," said Mufasa, "as long as you remember that everything you see exists together in a delicate balance – a great Circle of Life. As the King, you will have to take your place in the Circle and help to preserve that balance."

"Father," said Simba, looking out towards the horizon. "What's that shadowy place out there?"

Mufasa turned to his son. "That is beyond our borders," he said. "You must *never* go there."

Just then Zazu arrived.
"Sire!" he said. "Hyenas have
crossed into the Pride Lands!"

Quickly the King ordered
Zazu to take Simba home.

"Oh, please let me come with
you, Father," Simba begged.

"No," said Mufasa. "It's too
dangerous!" And he rushed away.

A short time later Simba was scrambling up Pride Rock when he met Scar, who was sunning himself on a ledge.

"Uncle Scar, guess what?" said Simba. "I'm going to be king one day, and Father's just shown me our whole kingdom!"

"Really?" said Scar. A nasty plan began to take shape in his mind. "Did he show you what's beyond the northern border?"

"No," Simba admitted sadly. "He said I must never go there."

"And he's absolutely right!" Scar declared. "Only the *bravest* lions go there. An elephant graveyard is no place for a young prince!"

Wow! thought Simba. *So that's what's out there – an elephant graveyard! That sounds exciting!*

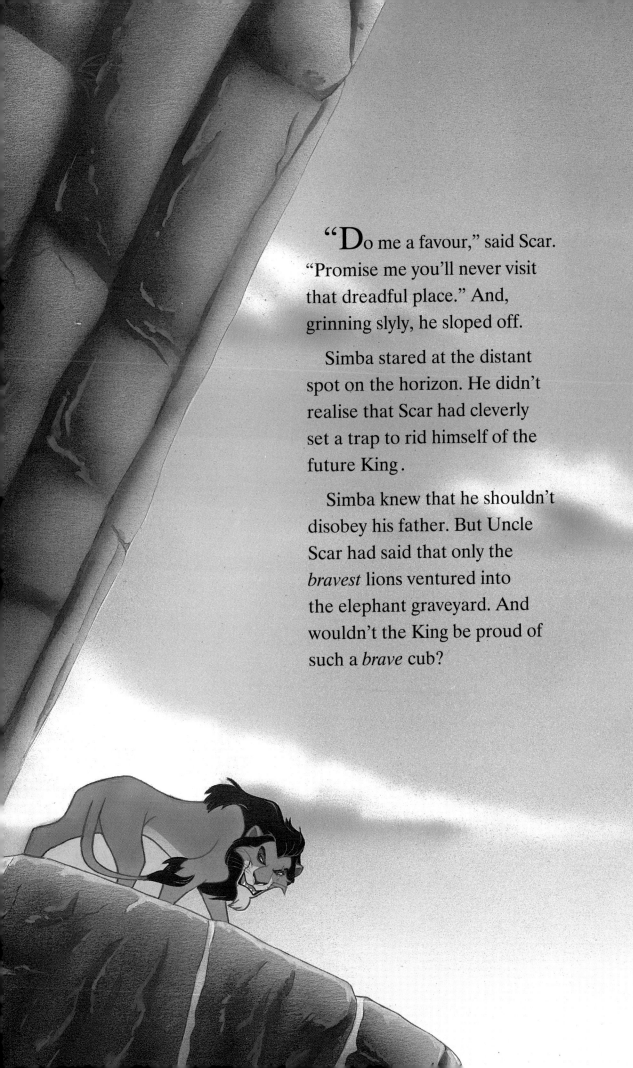

"Do me a favour," said Scar. "Promise me you'll never visit that dreadful place." And, grinning slyly, he sloped off.

Simba stared at the distant spot on the horizon. He didn't realise that Scar had cleverly set a trap to rid himself of the future King.

Simba knew that he shouldn't disobey his father. But Uncle Scar had said that only the *bravest* lions ventured into the elephant graveyard. And wouldn't the King be proud of such a *brave* cub?

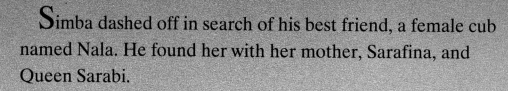

Simba dashed off in search of his best friend, a female cub named Nala. He found her with her mother, Sarafina, and Queen Sarabi.

"Mother," he said to Sarabi, "I just heard about this really terrific place. Can Nala and I go, please?"

"Where is this 'really terrific place', Simba?" his mother asked.

"Er, near the waterhole," Simba lied. He knew Uncle Scar would be angry if he told.

"All right," said Sarabi, "as long as Zazu goes with you."

Oh, no! thought Simba. *Zazu will spoil everything!*

"We've got to get rid of Zazu!" Simba whispered to Nala. "We're going to an elephant graveyard, not the waterhole!"

Zazu looked back at them. "Just look at the two of you, telling secrets!" he said. "Your parents will be thrilled. You're going to be married one day, you know!"

"I can't marry Nala!" Simba protested. "She's my *friend*! When I'm the King, I'll do just as *I* please!"

"With that attitude," said Zazu sternly, "you won't be a very good king!"

Simba laughed at Zazu.
"I can't wait to be king!" he
shouted, darting into a herd
of zebras. Nala followed, and
the pair escaped from Zazu in
the maze of striped animals.

"It worked! We lost him!" boasted Simba. "Now we can look for the elephant graveyard!"

"I think we've found it," said Nala. "Look!"

In the mist ahead of them they could see a huge elephant skull.

"It's really creepy," said Nala.

"Come on," said Simba. "Let's check it out."

But Zazu caught up with them. "Leave here *immediately*!" he squawked. "This is beyond the boundary of the Pride Lands and we're all in great danger!"

"I laugh in the face of danger!" boasted Simba. "Ha, ha!"

"Hee, hee!" came the reply – from the elephant skull! And out of the eyeholes sprang three drooling hyenas.

"Well, well, well," said one hyena. "What have we got here, Banzai?"

"I don't know, Shenzi," answered another. "What do you think, Ed?"

Ed, the third hyena, just licked his lips.

Baring their fangs, the hyenas crept towards the intruders. When Shenzi threatened Nala, Simba smacked the hyena across her nose.

"Ow!" screeched Shenzi. "I'll get you for that!"

"Nala, run!" yelled Simba, as the hyenas bounded after them.

The cubs found themselves trapped inside a gigantic rib cage. Fangs gleaming, the angry hyenas advanced towards Simba.

Suddenly a giant paw struck Shenzi, sending her and the other hyenas hurtling into a pile of bones.

"Don't you ever come near my son again!" Mufasa roared as the hyenas fled.

Later, when they were alone, Mufasa said to Simba, "I'm very disappointed in you."

Simba looked very ashamed. "I was just trying to be brave like you, Father," he said.

"I'm only brave when I have to be," said Mufasa. "Being brave doesn't mean you go looking for trouble."

Overhead, stars began to twinkle. "Father, we'll always be together, won't we?" asked Simba, as he trotted beside Mufasa.

"Simba, let me tell you something my father told me," said Mufasa gently. "Look up at the sky. The great kings of the past look down at us from those stars. They will always be there to guide you – and so will I."

That night Scar went to see the hyenas. "You idiots!" he shouted. "I gave you the perfect opportunity to get rid of that pest, Simba – and you could have killed Mufasa, too!"

"Kill Mufasa?" exclaimed Shenzi. "Are you kidding?"

"No, you mongrels," replied Scar. "Listen to me! I have another plan…"

Next morning Scar led Simba down into a deep gorge.

"What are we doing here, Uncle Scar?" Simba asked.

"Your father has a marvellous surprise for you," Scar explained. "Just wait here while I fetch him."

And Scar dashed off – to tell the hyenas it was time to put his plan into action.

A herd of wildebeest were grazing peacefully in the gorge. As soon as the hyenas got the signal from Scar, they charged into the herd. Startled, the animals began to stampede.

Simba, right in the path of the huge beasts, clawed his way onto a branch. As the herd thundered past, the branch suddenly cracked!

Nearby, Mufasa and Zazu noticed the dust rising from the gorge.

"Mufasa!" Scar yelled, appearing from behind a rock. "Quick! There's a stampede – and Simba's trapped down there!"

"I'm coming, son!" shouted Mufasa, leaping into the gorge. He grabbed the terrified cub in his mouth and carried him to safety.

43

But Mufasa himself was knocked down by a galloping wildebeest. Injured and in pain, he struggled to pull himself out of the gorge.

"Scar, help me," he panted as he neared the top.

Scar leaned over. "Long live the King!" he snarled viciously. Then, with a deadly shove, he flung Mufasa back to the bottom of the gorge.

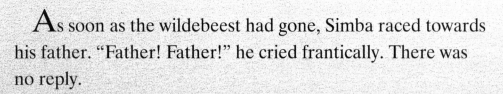

As soon as the wildebeest had gone, Simba raced towards his father. "Father! Father!" he cried frantically. There was no reply.

Sobbing, Simba nuzzled Mufasa's still body. The great Lion King was dead.

Scar appeared beside Simba. "What have you done?" he said menacingly.

"It was an accident!" the cub wailed.

"If the King hadn't tried to save you, he'd still be alive," Scar snarled. "You must run away and *never* return!"

Heartbroken and confused, Simba fled.

49

Scar immediately sent the hyenas after Simba, with orders to kill him. Simba outran them to the edge of a plateau and then leapt into a tangle of thorns.

Defeated, the hyenas abandoned the chase. "But we'll get you if you ever come back!" they called after the young cub.

Certain that Simba had been killed, Scar returned with the news to Pride Rock.

Sarabi, Nala and the other lionesses wept bitterly when they heard that the King and the Prince were both dead. Scar slowly ascended Mufasa's throne. "It is with a heavy heart that I become your new king," he said solemnly.

Rafiki, shaking his head in disbelief, sadly walked away from the Pride.

Simba, injured and exhausted, had stumbled across the blazing, hot African wasteland. At last, unable to go any further, he fell to his knees and fainted.

Hungry vultures circled above him, ready to swoop down for their afternoon meal.

When Simba opened his eyes, the burning sun and the vultures had gone, and a meerkat and a warthog were standing over him.

"You nearly died," said the warthog. "We saved you!"

"Thanks for your help," Simba said, standing up shakily. He started to leave.

The meerkat called after the cub, "Where are you from, kid?"

"It doesn't matter," Simba replied miserably. "I can't go back there."

"Then stay here with us!" cried the meerkat. "My name's Timon, and this is Pumbaa. Take my advice, kid – put your past behind you. *Hakuna matata* – no worries! That's what we say!"

Simba decided to stay in the jungle with his new friends. As Timon offered Simba some juicy bugs to eat, the meerkat said, "You'll see, you'll love it here. Just remember – *hakuna matata*!"

The years passed happily for Simba, and he grew into a strong and handsome young lion.

One morning he heard his friends shouting for help. Hurrying to them, he found Pumbaa caught beneath a fallen tree. Timon was trying to protect him from a hungry, young lioness.

Simba rushed forward. As he wrestled with the lioness, she stared at him.

"Simba?" she said, hesitantly.

"Nala?" he replied.

The lions hugged, overjoyed to have found each other again.

"Hey, what's going on?" asked Timon.

Simba laughed and introduced Nala to his friends. She smiled politely but she couldn't stop staring at Simba. Finally she said, "Everyone thinks you're dead. Scar told us about the stampede."

"What else did he tell you?" Simba asked cautiously.

"What else matters?" Nala exclaimed. "You're alive! And that means you're the King!"

"*King?*" cried Timon and Pumbaa in surprise.

Excusing themselves, Simba and Nala strolled through the jungle. "Scar let the hyenas take over the Pride Lands," Nala said. "Things are terrible. There's no food, no water. Simba, you've got to come back and help."

"I can't go back," Simba insisted.

"Why not?" Nala asked, bewildered. "Simba, what's happened to you? Why are you hiding from your responsibilities? What would your father think?"

"My father is dead," said Simba, and he turned and walked away.

That night, while the others slept, Simba gazed up at the star-filled sky. *I can never go back*, he thought. *How could I show my face in the Pride?* "And even if I did go back," he said aloud, "it wouldn't do any good. I'm not you, Father. I never will be."

Suddenly, as if from nowhere, a wizened old baboon appeared beside the young lion.

"Who are you?" Simba asked.

"The question is… who are *you*?" replied the baboon.

"I know your father," he went on. "Come. I will take you to him. Just follow Rafiki. He knows the way."

Amazed, Simba followed the baboon to a still, clear pool. "Look down there," Rafiki told him.

But all Simba could see was his own reflection.

"Look *harder*," Rafiki encouraged him.

A breeze rippled the water. When the pool became still once more, Simba stared down at the face of his father.

"You see?" said Rafiki. "He lives in *you*!"

Suddenly Simba heard a voice calling his name. He looked up – and there in the stars was the image of his father.

"Look inside yourself, Simba," said the image. "You must take your place in the Circle of Life. Remember who you are. You are my son, and the one true King. Remember…"

The vision faded, and Simba was alone.

Next morning Rafiki came to see Nala, Timon and Pumbaa. "The King has returned," he told them.

"What do you mean?" asked Timon, worried.

"Simba has gone back to Pride Rock to challenge his uncle," exclaimed Nala happily. "I'm going with him!"

"Me, too!" said Pumbaa.

Timon hesitated, upset at losing his friend. But finally he decided to follow Simba to Pride Rock as well.

73

Ahead of them all, Simba was crossing into his homeland. Everywhere he looked he saw devastation and ruin. For a moment he paused, wondering if he should go back while he still could. Then he felt a fresh wind and saw rain clouds gathering on the horizon. His hope restored, he went on.

Soon Nala, Pumbaa and Timon reached the Pride Lands. As they approached Pride Rock, they saw some hyenas. Timon and Pumbaa stayed behind to distract them while Nala went to find the lionesses. Simba forged on alone, searching for his uncle.

Meanwhile, at Pride Rock, Scar carried on his reign of terror.

"Where is your hunting party?" he bellowed at Sarabi.

"There is nothing to hunt," she replied. "The herds have moved on. Our only hope is to leave Pride Rock."

"We're not going anywhere," growled Scar.

"Then you are sentencing us to death," said Sarabi.

"So be it!" said Scar. "I am the King, and I make the rules!"

"If you were half as good a king as Mufasa was…" Sarabi began. Enraged, Scar struck her, and she fell.

All at once a mighty roar echoed through the rocks. Scar whirled round and saw a great lion before him.

"Mufasa?" he gasped. "No! It can't be! You're dead!" Scar backed away, terrified. He thought he was seeing a ghost. "Why are you here?" he whimpered. "Go away! Leave me alone!"

But even though many years had passed, Sarabi still recognised her son. "Simba, you're alive!" she said quietly.

"Yes, and I have come to reclaim my kingdom," Simba declared. "Step down, Scar."

Scar laughed. "Well, I would, of course," he said, "but there is one little problem." He gestured towards the hyenas.

The hyenas went straight for Simba. He tried to fight them off, but he was outnumbered. They forced him to the edge of the cliff.

"Enough!" Scar cried. He padded over and looked down at Simba, who was struggling to keep his hold on the rock.

"Now, where have I seen this before?" Scar sneered. "Oh, yes. I remember. This is the way your father looked just before I killed him."

At last Simba knew the truth, and with renewed strength, he drew himself up and leapt at Scar.

As Scar called in the hyenas, Nala and the lionesses arrived, along with Timon and Pumbaa. With fury, they attacked the hyenas and began driving them away.

As the groups clashed, lightning struck the dry grass of the plain. The wind swept huge flames towards Pride Rock.

Simba saw Scar crawling up Pride Rock. Dodging the blaze, Simba dashed up the steep face and trapped Scar at the edge.

"Please don't hurt me," Scar begged. "The hyenas killed your father. They're the enemy, Simba. I'm your family!"

Simba paused for a moment, then said, "Run away, Scar. Run away and *never* return!"

Scar started to slink away. Suddenly he turned and lunged at Simba. Acting swiftly, Simba hurled Scar off the cliff. The angry hyenas, waiting at the bottom of the cliff, killed their defeated master.

As rain began to fall, Simba climbed to the top of Pride Rock. The clouds parted, revealing a sky gleaming with stars. Simba roared triumphantly, and all who heard him felt a surge of hope rise within them.

Soon, under the rule of a wise and brave king, the Pride Lands flourished. The herds returned and food was plentiful once more.

Then one day the animals gathered from across the plain to celebrate the birth of King Simba and Queen Nala's new son.

As Rafiki held the cub high over Pride Rock, Simba thought of his father and remembered his love and wisdom. Then, with happiness in his heart, he welcomed his son to the unbroken Circle of Life.